Kelsey,

Thank you
The first edit copy of
my book. I hope this
inspires you to keep
fighting through every
hard time that fronts you!!

NEIL BARBER

Everything HUMAN in ME
VOLUME 1

authorHOUSE®

AuthorHouse™ UK
1663 Liberty Drive
Bloomington, IN 47403 USA
www.authorhouse.co.uk
Phone: 0800.197.4150

© 2018 Neil Barber. All rights reserved.

No part of this book may be reproduced, stored in a retrieval system, or transmitted by any means without the written permission of the author.

Published by AuthorHouse 09/28/2018

ISBN: 978-1-5462-9884-7 (sc)
ISBN: 978-1-5462-9885-4 (e)

Print information available on the last page.

Any people depicted in stock imagery provided by Getty Images are models, and such images are being used for illustrative purposes only. Certain stock imagery © Getty Images.

This book is printed on acid-free paper.

Because of the dynamic nature of the Internet, any web addresses or links contained in this book may have changed since publication and may no longer be valid. The views expressed in this work are solely those of the author and do not necessarily reflect the views of the publisher, and the publisher hereby disclaims any responsibility for them.

Introduction

As I was growing up, I lost myself along the way, never knowing who I was truly meant to be. I struggled with dyslexia from a early age which caused me to feel isolated as I had difficulties communicating with my peers. My experience of learning to adapt and develop the necessary skills to successfully gain my academic qualifications, led me to help others. This ability gave me a very professional career of 14 Years in the care industry.

Now at the ripe old age of 33 after needing to stop work due to ill health, I have accidentally stumbled across a way of expressing my emotions through words. I never knew, I possessed this very rare talent, or the power to help others through my own life journey with words. This concern inspired me to write about my journey with a chronic disease that not many understand or see. It also describes the many journeys that I have travelled through in life that everyone will be able to relate to.

For I want people to understand and learn, what it feels like to walk in someone else's shoes. We all struggle daily with our own issues, although many do not look at the big picture. Living with a chronic disease or being a carer, family member of someone makes life all that more demanding. We sometimes need a gentle reminder that sometimes these issues, are out of our control and not of their own making.

This thinking led me start watching the world and the people I viewed daily. Through the love, loss, pain and many lessons life throws at people throughout the world. It gave me the insight to start writing about what I observed from a perspective of concern and respect for many who suffer in silence. With every word I wrote they naturally formed into poems.

I hope "Everything Human In Me" will give everyone who lives there life in silence a voice, the courage and inspiration to battle on, or stand up and tell the world of there hardest times. With my poems, I hope to show the human race there are no two different people. We all experience the same hardships in life. Because you and I are really the same in many ways.

On The Edge Of Life

Falling from the sky faster than light,
I woke in a room of sea blue uniforms.
What has become of the
young man in his prime?

I was standing by his side,
gazing right through him,
Wondering what events brought him here,
I started scanning the room,
I had become invisible to the
traffic of sea blue uniforms,
My ears fortified against all
noise that once was,
A tube hung from my mouth that
once held such vibrant remarks,
Detached, I had become from
my eyes vision before me.

Pondering to my invisible
who this could be,
Suddenly, a sharp pain rose from inside,
It hit me with such pace and venom,
This was I the young man in his prime,

So pale I had drained as I
lay so helpless inside,
A coma of peace stands by my side,
Thinking now my time had come
to meet the maker of me,
But with such haste I gasped for breath,
Then woke from the nightmare inside.

Lost Love

I woke today again with
you on my thoughts,
It was a struggle to fix my
sights on anything else,
So I came to the one place in
this world, I feel at peace,
Where the land meets the sea, but
constant breezes warm my soul,
With time maybe, I will be
able to heal myself,
Although, I will always carry amazing
memories with me of you forever,
I regret not loving you harder
everyday, By my side you were,
You will always hold that special
place in my heart of hearts.

Remembrance

A bugle plays once more
the last stand we hear,
Streams of poppies fill their arms,
We remember all the fallen from
past but also present days.

All the valiant men that gave life
for the freedom of our country,
With a reef in hand veterans pay one
final salute, to fallen comrades in arms,
As brothers they once stood, but now only
respect to pay for the sacrifice given.

Flags lowered to half mast as
a sign we never forget,
The world stands still for a minute,
So we all remember who they were,
With pride in our hearts we have
become eternally grateful,
For everything you gave,
So long may your legacies live
on in the nation you inspired.

*"I carry my scars with pride for all to see,
As they are constant reminders
of the battles I've won."*

Once Again

It's come again so soon,

why has this become me again?
No sooner I healed it's reared
that ugly head again,
Have legs again that have
become an alien form,
A twitch I feel strike down my face,
This suffering inside once felt dull,
However, beats with an immense
pace with such haste,
I have become stuck again in this
whirlwind of this vile disease,
It has swallowed me whole
of whom I become.
But know the struggle has
become inside once more,
With no slowing down insight,
Still remains raging on inflicting
so much destruction
of the former man in me,
A shadow again descends down
on control I once saw.

Will a easier time show at last?

Although, first the insects must
leave my destroyed body,
Then I might find the strength
once more to face this world,
So until that time I will find
comfort in shadows,
My last hope has left my future for now.

Never Before

Never before has a love shown
like an engulfing flame,
Ripping through ones spirit.

Never before have he
wanted her so much,
That she spends an eternity
running through my heart.

Never before have he seen
a future with the one,
He would die for in the rest of one's life.

Never before has he shown all his flaws,
However, he shall forever more to you.

Never before has he been
attracted to such beauty,
Which stands right before his eyes.

Never before has he felt this much love,
Thou shall show you everyday
what one means to me.

Never before has he found someone,
That completes me in every way you do.

Never before has he wanted love so pure,
Until the day you walked through the door.

Hero

A hero once stood, but the world
has forgotten them now,
So a solemn man stands alone, whilst
rain pours on his distorted soul.

Where has he come from?
Or, where does he go?

No one knows, but only him of
whom he has become,
The expressions that bears on
his face tell a million stories,
But pain that displays in his sombre eyes,
tell of the lose he has suffered inside.

The ghastly world keeps on spinning,
but he shall remain still inside,
Every memory flashes so lucid before
his eyes, for none he wants to see,
As life drains from his exhausted body
standing in a mine filled once more.

There he remains standing as still
like ice remembering them all,
From days that have past but
there shall be one final salute,
For his fallen brother in arms
as the world spins on by.

"Desperation of the human, Lays in this Unforgiving world...."

My Enemy

I close my eyes for a minute,
nearly feeling normal,
My mind is shattered and broken inside,
This thing I have controls
my every thought,
Like a deluded illness running free inside.

I try to brush it aside, then live again,
For it stops me in my tracks furthermore,
As It will not beat me, only makes
my mind go crazy inside,
No rational thoughts to clear my
doubt of suspicious intent,
This thing I have rampages on inside.

My own worst enemy I have become,
Which I hold at the core of me,
Until this day my demons
will carry on there fury,
A war zone my mind has become,

Colours so vivid still in pictures
of the destruction in me,
Slowly my mind repairs, but the scars
of damage will stay within me,
So for now, I must live to fight another day.

Noticed

Don't stutter she noticed you,
Stand as still like a statue,
she might pass by,
She perceives all the colours
of affection with her eyes,
Such beauty she carries, so
vibrant on her shoulders.

Never before have you seen
someone so bold,
Her graceful stance of
attractiveness, invites you in,
The hands she holds glide through
any storm, that fronts her,
A need of impulse rises from
inside your vessel.

But you can only gaze upon
her unknown spirit,
The craving you hold to chase her,
Turns you into a frenzy of passion,
The one you must have she has become.

Hope

New found hope crushed out of every
bone, in her uninhabited body,
The deluded plague rages
in her own mind,
Never she thought this shall
become her life,
Closer she looks but the world
remains these four walls,
Suddenly she thought, she may
never hold her dearest loves,
So tears roll from her empty
spheres of ice.

A wife once, a mother isolated,
from a home she holds so dear,
No hope seen at every new
sunrise in this desolate place,
A freedom declined for the
innocents of this caged mother,
Prayers remain unanswered
by a powerful nation,
A woman denied every hope of
happiness in this cruel world.

*"My spirit will fly high on winds,
Carrying me to brighter places."*

Relapse

As I lay in bed,
My legs don't feel mine,
A marathon I've just run,
But no finish line insight,
A lighting bolt I feel,
That times has come again,
It's ghastly head has reared once more.

As I battle with the discomfort,
I fix my sights on my strength inside,
Struggling to my weary legs again,
As I gaze in the mirror,
A shadow of the former man
I once was, I saw.

What's destined for me I do not know,
But the war inside continues on,
Knowing, this I will fight on,
This nasty illness will not
ruin what I have inside.

So I now know, I might merely exist,
But with this vile disease,
I can still truly exist,
The legs that were not mine,
start dancing once more,
The day has come I must face my foes,
As this has become my only friend.

Dream

She touched my heart,
I have become what she desires inside,
He touched her soul, so she has
become what I dreamed of,
My soul mate I have found
as well as become,
A true friend I once dreamed
of, I have found,
So perfect in every way with scars insight.

She sits but stares so intense her love,
My soul flickers then dances
with her insight,
Her one true north I hold for her,
A love so pure I have found but become,
The rage of passion in each of our hearts,
For two hearts left dwelling
places have become one.

The rock of my life she has become
to dwindle away the pain insight,
A future show bright now shines on us,

The resting place for my heart
she holds with hers,
My one true love, I want forever,
Until my dying breath, I will hold forever.

Missing Mother

Tormented by her own captures,
seen by the millions,
But she only becomes her own torment,
by the loss of her small child,
About time people sat up listening,
to the story of a missing mother.

Only she feels the pain that
slowly rips inside her heart,
The mental anguish she feels,
with every passing thought,
A grief she holds so clear,
for her one desire,
To slowly embrace the one thing
she wants to hold so near,
The love seen in pictures so pure,
then seen by the millions.

She still sits isolated in a cage,
In a land not her home,
Why has she been left so long,
to become her own torment?
For a society fighting for the
freedom, of a missing mother.

*"Maybe I am too damaged to be loved,
My demolished shell to hard to mend."*

Vile Disease

I stumble, I can feel the thousand
strangers eyes pierce through me,
She steadies me but my legs
don't work no more,
Slowly she walks beside me
her grip getting tighter,
I stumble again, this vile
disease has a grip of me,
I Fight against it with all my might,
but no more does my body.

This horrid disease controls me
now, but only for a while.

My head held high I reach for my aids,
But my hands don't want to work no more,
Still the thousand strangers
eyes pierce through me,
A cripple I fell destined by
this vile disease.

I once stood a man with pride inside,
Now I have become broken within,
This vile disease control me
know, but only for a while.

Soon the light will come, then at that time.

I will bid my oldest friend farewell.

Love

Follow me to the brink of life,
with your tenderness,
I will show you everything in my life,
Be careful though, my love.

It might become so bright, because
this you taught me of love,
Vivid colours now merge into one,
constantly telling our story.

Fond memories of years together,
I hold secretly in me,
Never let this emotion dye inside of us,
For I have many more years
of love to give you.

Grief

Stay with me I am so cold,
Just a little bit longer my beloved,
A few seconds is all we have left.

Close your eyes precious,
Remembering all our glory days.

Slowly succumb to whatever
it has in store,
Embrace it for this shall be
your next chapter.

For all our time together,
I have always cherished you.
But for the rest of time, I will still love you.

My hearts breaking with sorrow
for, I will never hold you again.

"Blood flows down the river, For love in our hearts sometimes bleeds out."

Depression

A young statue of a man raised
above the world to see,
Pinned to one spot by stone from within,
Lost between two worlds he had become,
No time for wondering or
even to contemplate,
How did he ever struggle to here,
No sight left for seeing the
wonders of our world insight.

So touch no more from his stone hands,
A slumber in the state of mind
shall show once more,
But once more a yearning he
feels to be semi normal,
A sudden move the once solid
stone shows a crack at last,
Colour returns with such clarity
defining everything insight,
A depression that once was lifts finally,
Which shows many a crack of the
scars in this distorted soul.

Breathe

Let's breathe together with our lives,
Inhale all of me in filling your lungs,
In return I will breath all of you in,
So they can soar together
like never before.

Filling my body with so much joy,
Then gentle touch my face so, I
always remember your touch.

But then I will navigate your body,
touching every inch of you.

Delicately place your lips on mine,
so I know how soft they feel.
Then let me run my fingers through
your hair, so I know how it falls.
But let me be the one that pulls
you closer, on to your toes.

Mothers Freedom

She has lost her life with freedom
insight, in a world she trusted.
Now her only friend, these steel
rods of iron have become,
But still time rolls on for this caged mother.

So shall remain in a hostile
land with torture Insight,
No day passes without pain in her heart,
for loved ones she holds so close.

As days roll into one there
remains no end insight,
Fear becomes her at every
thought of freedom,
The hope of being close to loved
ones slowly dying inside,
There is a sadness that lays so deep,
for a daughter she once adored.

As shall only see light through the bars,
Which hold her from a life she once lived,
So this struggle of her life will carry
on, until the world takes note.

"Tonight you are everything, Tomorrow you might become nothing…"

Demons Within

Creeping on the haze of a shadow,
No one ever wants monsters
lurking in the dark,
But monsters are demons of
every person insight,
Just lingering waiting for
the chaos to start.

Many have seen there demons within,
But few ever let them roam
so freely outside,
The ones that play are peaceful in soul,
So friends they must become
to survive inside.

The monsters now seem not so tragic,
As I grasp there hand running
happily around me,
Soon will come the time to
spread their wings then fly.

Entice

Never has he seen such
vibrant beauty before,
So shall stare right into her
slowly dying heart,
Possessed by the desire of love.

He tries in every way to
entice her longing gaze,
So damaged she has become
that no man sees,
Therefore, his eyes full of love for
her, sees the scars within.

He felt the cold in her voice
descend over his soul,
But never was he giving up
the chase for her,
As he saw a loving soul held
behind barriers of steel.

She must be conquered then
shown love once more,

Then one day he saw a glowing
warmth, crawling out from within her,
Finally a new found desire that
she wanted had rose,
For smiles like, the brightest stars
beamed across her once sombre face.

My Child

Every day my child it hurts,
For I have been stupid but only the once.

I remember the last time, we
laid eyes on each other,
Like it was only yesterday, which
was to many years ago.

I should never have let you
go from my side,
But will be reminded daily by
the sorrow in my life.

Through pictures I see of you growing,
I gather some warmth
knowing you are loved.

But the pain will always remain dear child,
For one day I hope we meet again.

*"Take me back, Now take me back
to when life was no worry…"*

Crushed Shell

Once a storm, now grows into
a full blown hurricane.
The cold creeps up inwards,
running in my veins.
Crippling every move deep inside,

The strength one needs slowly dying
in ones, weary depleted limbs.
Some courage left slowly bleeds,
out of every possible orifice.

With no sign that I may be
strong enough to swim,
These choppy waters once more,
So needs the strength of dear loved
ones, to pull me through once again.

The man stands before me, with
pain in his sombre eyes.

Just became me again.

With the dull ache inside this
crushed shell, of this man.
Which has come to only exist for now,

Shall I say it has beat one?

But my brain fights with every
movement inside,
My mind is the courage,
Whilst love will only make me
fight for another day.

Captured

A girl sat across from me who
saw everything I was,
Deep in colour whilst mysteriously
dancing eyes, you held from there.

Your smile spoke a hundred
feelings to me,
But your eyes spoke a million times more.

Your laugh was infectious beyond
any yearning, I held for you.

I remember longing to wrap
myself in your loving web,
Taking one deep breath in whilst
you, breathed life through me.

So gentle your voice sang
every time you came near,
A warm glow shone over your
entire surroundings,
Outlining your soul to me.

Then the way you run your
hands through your hair,
So affectionately towards me.

Shall one say this was the day you
captured then stole ones heart.

Caged Mother

She sits in her cage unconditional
love flows through her dying heart,
For a small child plays on every
heartstring that she remembers so fondly,
A child is lost running free in her
soul creating every tear insight,
The strength she needs to find pulls
on her every tormented thought.

She must survive another day
in this nightmare place,
Longing for one last embrace from
her crushed life she plays,
A broken mind sits by her side, no
one listens so depression rages on.

Thoughts of living through this
nightmare destroy her day by day,
As the missing piece of her
jigsaw lays inside her,
The small child which has become her.

*"A little bit of you, Trapped
all inside of me....."*

Uncontrolled Destiny

The uncontrolled destiny of one's life,
Thrown into terminal by a chronic disease.

Lingering in the depths waiting to strike,
with such force then venom it's friend.

Such devastation caused by
crippling of every signal inside,
All short circuits shown
although, no repair insight.

Many seen before destroyed to
just merely existing vessels,
For the battle no one sees of
the chronic disease within,
That only the host knows, the
long fought war shall remain.

Desire

Love grows in a barren place, that
none have ever before touched.
A bleak heart slowly brought back
from the brink of darkness,
That's shown for to long.

Shall one say a love nurtured by you,
With the love that has become
because of you.

A overwhelming desire shows at
every look from inside you,
Nevertheless, every minute of every day,
The need for you drives me to madness.

My love for you grows every day
so one will love thee more,
As I savour every memory of you,
my mind becomes active again.

The thought of loving you more excites
my ever aching heart strings,
You have become me for now until forever,
I shall hold your love so near to me
so, As I will never let go of you.

500 Days

Five hundred days it has been
since she last held her rock,
The so called life once led, by
her now becomes a dream.

A child she held so tight with love,
a stranger she has become.
All the colours of happier days
fade into one vivid grey haze.

No sun insight to bring a close from
this constant dreaded place,
A world outside stands beside
you for one we have become.

Close one's eyes for a minute
so that's how dark,
It has become in the shattered
mother's mind.

All our strength we pass to you
with hope of justice insight,
But all our love we give thee, for
the strength you need to fight.

"Time can slowly mend you, But real love can make you fly again......"

Kiss Goodbye

Now hear the silent 2.3 million voices cry,
For there invisible illness continually
discriminated against,
Judgement thrown from
every angel insight,
The world needs to know of this heavy
burden they carry so proudly.

So we will kiss goodbye to
it from every nation,
Then hopefully be granted a
cure to rid the world of this,
But until that time we will
unite as one family,
With squads plotted all over the world,
For all to see what amazing
people these are.

Fragile Heart

Rip it out of me dear, tear it out from me.

Now stamp all over it, nothing
has come to matter.

Crush it under your heel, I
don't need it no more.

See I told you it was fragile, make it bleed.

Make it ooze red, See I am
but nothing to you.

Now pick it up then give it back, For
it is the piece of me I gave to you.

Now leave walk away from me,
Then never turn back to see me.

For I am broken by you, see I don't
need for a heart in this cold world.

Be Her

Be her hope,
Be her strength,
Be her voice as she cannot be heard.
Be the love in her daughter's heart,
Be the compass she needs by her side.

Be as one for her freedom now,
Be the reason we will never forget,
Be the fighting world they never expected.

Be the wind to carry her home,
Be the sun to brighten her day,
Be her reason for never giving up,
Be the story for all the world to hear,
Be together for the missing mother.

*"Love will find you under any dark cloud,
Returning the light to you life so
we can see once more…"*

Orange Warrior

Hear my battle cry from the warrior inside,
Listen to my beating heart of war drums,
Watch as I slay everything
evil inside out of me.

The courage I possess will see
me rise whenever I fall,
My pride only I will carry on my shoulders,
Such strength I will show at
anything thrown in my way,
For I am an orange warrior.

My Prayer

Like a prayer, I hold so
near she's become.
One I shall not be parted from,
The conviction of his heart is her,
Which she holds everything of
him, with her heart so near.

Never has his damaged core seen love,
Nevermore, has destiny in
him been so clear.

A infectious desire she has become,
The final chapter of his life
he craves in her,
A force so strong she holds
so close with him,
For this dwelling heart she
wears with pride.

He shall continue to fix with stars insight,
A love with honoured has engulfed him,
Her passion has been imprinted
in his heart by her.

The darkness that once was
now light fills beside him,
The gentleness of his soul
only matured by her,
A guide she has formed for him.
With love I only see in her.

Don't Forget

Kneel down touch the ground,
I can feel you there, only not in my arms.

Wait for me now, I will be
following you soon.
Don't forget me so we can
find each other again.

The only time I see you is in my dreams,
Come back to me then hold
me tight once more,
For this life drained to emptiness
since you departed.

*"We were born with two different souls,
That ignite into the wildest
fires when near....."*

The Game

So the game has started once more,
A paranoid presence I shall feel from here,
Every feeling has slowly died
through the destruction of me,
Finally darkness covers my body,
No figures I see through light that shows,
The fragile state of my mind
returns once more.

A game I don't want to play
no more rages on,
The cry for help comes from deep within,
A hurtful pain that needs to fade so fast,
Why has this become me again,
I don't want this to be me no more.

Slowly I am dying inside
my tormented mind,
A cold metal presses against my skin,
Do I hesitate to inflict more pain,
Or should I watch my veins become death,
I need to find some strength.

Dream

So close to me I feel her warmth,
She holds me near so I can see all,
I notice burning love inside her soul,
Until this day a dream she was.

Now that dream breaths with me,
Eyes alight, Which I have
never seen before.

So in return a piece of me,
she will see but hold.
With a time so precious, we shall
share in hearts of ours.

We have become every waking
hour for one another,
For these two hearts we hold as one,

The lasting dream met by love we found,
With becoming the dreaming
desire for each other.

New Born

I remember them eyes when
you first opened,
The smallest of fingers
clenched around my life.

The uncontrollable love that
raised from my roots,
With the way you nestled into my
arms, for the love you craved.

Followed your every milestone
with sheer delight,
Then danced with you in my arms
whilst, holding you so tight.

A love showed me in return
through your smallest heart,
Pictures I see of your smile
brings me such joy.

Then a promise i will make
to never give up,
For my child you shall be forever more.

*"Trust those who hold your
heart in content,
For these are the real bearers
of your happiness....."*

Psychosis

The eyes she holds start to flicker again,
It's time for the voices which are
steamed in ones deepmind,
To play so many different roles
that none never wants,
As a twitch strikes through
her surroundings, so the eyes
must role once more.

Many a person shows through
the vessel she has become,
At this time no one can help or even
come close to what she holds from here.

A violent tongue strikes through whilst
her eyes fill with such unforgivable rage,
The volatile storm she is passing through
picks up speed with so much haste,

An unconscious mind now shines,
For she has become so
peaceful with eyes closed.

Only then will her eyes return to the
former looks she holds so true.

Never Love Again

I will never love again, as you were
the last love, I ever wanted.
I will now be alone forever, Out
of respect to our love,
Which I will never be able to rid from me.

Like the sun will never leave the moon,
For I will never make you leave my heart,
As this has always been your place.

So let your memories fill me with joy,
Until the end of time,
Then I will be at peace knowing
you was my last love.

Darkness

A cold wind brushes his face,

Were has he come? For
where does he stand?

A familiar place I sense
but he looks so lost,
By his side stands a figure
of a lifeless person,
Once possessed by many a devil.

So still the air has become,
Colours fade into darkness,
Which clings close to his empty heart.

No one noticed him leaving
the world behind,
So torn by the fragile life he had led.

Critical of any craving pressed
against his mind,
With lasting disappointment from
failing at every step in life,

Belief that no good would come
to stand beside him.

So paranoia sits hand in hand
with every fleeting thought,
That present moment with
no sorrow insight,
Then joy fills his heart as devils flew by,
The time comes to live with
the magical world again.

"Teach me how to love again, For I have become so damaged inside…"

Mind Functions

I am sometimes lost, my mind
functions are broken.
You expect words but just get
silence as the only response.

I hear what you say but
never fully understand,
That's when I feel stupid
no questions I ask,
My mind knows stuff but
common conversations not.

I try so hard to speak openly
but no words I find,
Then become so vacant with
sorry the only remark I hold,
Constant frustration at my own
minds processes, I cannot cope.

Then goes on random detours about
any situation that fronts me in life.
For wandering eye show searching
for a answer with none I find,

Then beside you I am stupid, so my communication lacks conviction.

I ask numerous times then look at you,
With nothing I get back but emptiness.

Whole Again

I need to be whole again
which no more do I feel,
Each day I write thinking, ink
touching my pages will help.

For my body needs for something,
unsure of what anymore.

I felt myself lose my only compass, I
every found for this dreadful world.
However, then I always come
back to here my windy spot,
Where it has brought me so
much peace before.

This time just constant memories,
I see everywhere one looks.
I once had the most treasured thing,
This world could give the love of another,
But no more do I have.

Then I turn not knowing where to go,
For I never got to share.

One last tender kiss or warm embrace.

Death

The thought of death becoming
your only friend,
As cold metal presses against your skin,
Red starts to run from your
cold body walls.
Now comes the time, there
is no turning back.

You have travelled to far this
time with no saviour,
With the world's light before you,
getting dimmer but dimmer again.
Because what a waste of, a young
talented life they will write.

So close your eyes for one last time,
Though you will never know
as you depart this world.

"Never underestimate dreams, Dreams can define who we can be...."

Own Worst Enemy

One has become his own worst enemy,
A once honest man lost in his own web,
Spiralling out of control again for all to see,
This is not who he is, or
who he wants to be.

An honest man he wishes
back now more than ever,
The one that spoke with a truthful tongue,
Who never had a doubt in his
mind without true conviction.

Where have you gone old friend,
Come forth so you can take over control,
Until I find you again, this daily
struggle to live will carry on.

Just Remember

Just remember I saw you,
For the first time in life someone saw you.

I looked right into your beauty,
Stared right at your flaws,
Then stood by your side.

Through every hurdle you faced,
I was there holding your hand,
My grip getting tighter to make
sure you never fell,

Yet this chapter has closed,
Without being finished.

For now you have fallen, because
I'm not there no more,
Which has killed me everyday since.

Devils

Watch for the devils in life,
They dress like you and I.

There faces may seem pleasant,
Though their tempers will turn vulgar,
The tongues they hold hiss poison.

Be sure thought to watch for them eyes,
They shall draw you in then take you soul,
Then you shall become in their control.

With no returning to what you was before,
So now I tell you to step
carefully through this world.

"Universes can collide to bring two souls together, Never doubt that we are not destined to be together…"

Expressions

My expressions may look blank,
For that's because you never see,
What I have to fight with every day.

So bleak have become my emotions,
But so harden my strength
to rise another day,
For I have become my own savour
in the messed up world I see,
Now stand again with pride held high.

Then start to walk your road alone,
As sometimes no one ever
comes to understand,
What you fight with every day inside.

I See You

I see you but so quickly your gone,
I search behind every closed door,
I run back to the mirror,
I see you again that flickering smile.

Then you disappear from me.

I turn on every light to see you better,
But no more do I see you,
I feel your warm gentle breath on my neck.

Then you disappear once more.
Where are you now show yourself?

Then I hear the sound of you giggling,
But that's coming from deep within,
For what is happening in me,
Only you shall know the
memories left running in me.

Then you disappear once more.

Borrowed Time

We live on borrowed time everyday,
For not knowing when our story will end.

So love for today but hold
respect for yesterday,
For not knowing what
tomorrow has in store,
Scares us to sheer delight
or the most awful pain.

With a constant thought we
may never make it there,
So feel privileged for what you have today.

Then love everything in your life so deeply,
For tomorrow it may be removed.

*"Life holds a true meaning for everyone,
So travel on them endless
roads until you find it...."*

Troubled Times

Troubled times then bring terrible tremors,
For the telling eyes of suffering
they have held inside,
Speak for you like their is one story to tell.

The story of me with all my
unpleasant physical sensations,
That I hide from the world outside.

I should let them be free
soaring, like an eagle.
Which instead, I keep them
under lock and key.

I must release them from my
bodies prison walls,
Then the world will see my crippled
flaws, like the glitch in my matrix.

So now is the time, to show
the world my true colours,
For I have become that soaring eagle.

Embrace

Embrace me like no other
has done before,
Strip me back to bare raw bones.

Slowly rebuild my torn heart
with stitches of love,
Gentle piece back my
scared damage body.

Place your lips on mine bringing
back, the colours that once faded.

Touch my face so I know
your affection of love,
Then remember to take a
piece of my heart for you.

Now open my eyes so I can
see who saved me,
Then watch me as I embrace you.

My Journey

I open my eyes once more,
All the sorrow has left my side,
The scars remain for that's
the journey just walked,
A constant reminder of where I have been,
So each will tell a different story.

Of love but peace then pain,
Then I will lock them away,
For my heart needs to heal,
Because only I know when
the next chapter starts,
Then my heart will be ready
to open up once more.

*"Time can pass us by in
the blink of an eye,
So value the little things this
world has to give...."*

Flaws

See the sun breaks through me,
Exposing all my cracks,
Watch them glistening, then
dancing with the sun.

As they touch the ground
they bounce around,
To make a broken man shine,
For all to see the tears in
the body he carries,
Though he is proud of
those jagged edges,.

He wonders when his maker will fix him,
Or be stitched by the next found love,
For now he wishes to be
whole once more,
As he waits for the passing
of pain that once was.

Flames

Finally extinguished are the flames,
That drive us wild,
Smoke bellows from my skin,
Like the smoke signals of old,
While none come to his rescue,
Or saw the distress call.

So smouldering on carries my core,
Burning every sense alive.

From the shadows vultures appear,
To take what they shall,
From this devastated body.

Until there is but nothing left,
Of this exhausted life.

Piercing Eyes

I see a future so bright,
So free from dark,
I see who?
I've become by seeing your
eyes pierce through me.

A marvellous man stands before me,
So intensely passionate but free.

It has only been a short while
since you touched me,
Already I know my future lays beside you,
Now time stands still whilst
I breathe you in,
A whisper I hear of who I am within.

So gentle but nurturing that must be me,
Because you taught me to be free,
Which breathed new life through me.

Now I stand right before me,
the amazing man is me.
So this picture I see through
your piercing eyes Is me.

*"I could hold thee till my last breath,
But make sure you breathe into
me before I'm gone....."*

One

Shall one carry you,
When your legs become tired with life,
Then I feel one should hold your hand.

Through every approaching
storm you encounter,
One will then guide you to calmer waters,
Where you can recover from life stresses,
Then should one say you shall
never be left feeling lost,
Because one will be your
guide but compass.

Shall one be the light in your life,
Through every dark cave you must pass,
For this one will still be holding your hand.

Then one should love you more every day,
But sit you on the highest throne in life,
Which is beside me.

English Rose

Beautiful she is an English rose,
Flowered from within,
But not a compliment taken,
Just honest conviction of who she is.

Constant smiles found within
her aching soul,
But rarely her heart.

Sombre eyes speak of
years of pain inside,
Therefore, just one look
brought her back to life.

Life returned to every corner
of her dismantled soul,
Then floating on wings of
her new found love,
The up most ethereal she
carried through her heart,
An English rose she was dancing,
In the new sun of her former life.

Memories

My dear lady,
Why leave so many memories,
Scattered within me,
Every inch of my body,
You once touched remembers all.

I miss the gentleness,
I discovered in your delicate hands,
The way you smiled,

As you picked me up from
slumbers, I found in me.
It has not been long enough,
To stop putting ink on paper about you.

When the time comes,
I will remember fondly,
Every last word I wrote.

*"The distance between us
can never be measured,
Because I carry you with me
everywhere I travel...."*

Daughter

So much joyful delight,
You've brought our lives,
A small bundle of pure happiness you are,
You made us your parents,
As you shall be our daughter.

Never have we felt,
So much unconditional love,
For such a small bundle before.
As you have become our daughter.

The first time we held you,
In our arms we become complete,
Our little family we now hold so dear,
A life we now lead,
As you have become our daughter.

You have become the biggest part off,
For our love, for you will always shine.

As you have became our daughter.

Broken

Broken I am for that's me,
No repairs unable to bring me,
Back from where I am,
Lost right inside with no light,
To guide my way.

No hand to hold,
To help me from this unilluminated place,
So will carry on digging darker,
In one's own self loathing,
Slowly ripping out every emotion,
I once loved.

Darker but darker still I get,
Till I self explode inwards,
Causing greater mess,
For broken I am that's me.

All My Love

All my love I give thee,
You shall now hold as one,
Not a day shall pass,
That you must not hold my
heart with yours,
Nor will there be a time,
That I want to be apart from you.

A love for you has grown,
So fond in ones heart,
An embrace with you,
Is all that one really desires.

Nor does one ever want,
To become anything less in your eyes,
This man that has been moulded by you,
Never I want to lose,
For that man only exists for now.

"Stability of the human race balances in the unforgiving universe, Expanding all the time for us all to wonder what lies in wait, Moons come unveiling new wonders........"

Socially Awkward Boy

There I stand alone in a
corner of a vast corridor,
Whilst others travel so fast past me,
No one noticed yet this
damaged soul I possess,
The demons that rule my conscious
mind are better left unseen,
I look to myself I have no friends.

A socially awkward boy I see
staring through me.

I shut my eyes for a minute
then take a deep breath in,
These demons I must make my friends
but these demons might be me,
So I begin a journey not
sure what I will see,
The vast world lays before
me who will see me,
As I grow in age a few things change me.

A socially awkward boy I see
staring through me.

I feel no fear or pain, no more
my soul has left me,
Standing in a corner once
more a lifeless soul I see,
No emotions I feel in my eyes at
last there empty spheres of ice,
The cold person I have become is not me,
I shut my eyes once more
and who do I see.

A socially awkward boy I see
staring through me.

Guardian Angel

You came to me in the dark,
Unexpectedly in images, I
had seen ahead of time.

I never expected you to be resting
beside me like your doing,
Then time to time you catch
myself watching you sleep.

Like that peaceful angel you are,
For you are my guardian angel.

Homeless

The cold starts to creep into fragile bones,
He finds himself sitting against
the same old shop doorway,
While he gazes into a empty cup
which once filled with life,
His oldest friend stands on
all fours, by his side.

Every passing stranger ignores his
call for some warmth inside,
This was once a man with a bright future,
Slowly he was stripped of
everything he once was,
To the shell of the man he's become.

Now comes the time to survive
one more cold night,
Hoping that he will wake for another
day in this ghastly world,
So he remains in that old shop doorway
dreaming of a life that once was.

"These days become harder without your presence, Mornings I wake early but the Nights are long......."

Strength

Worsening are these symptoms I carry,
Just a ticking time bomb
waiting to implode,
It's time to stand tough with the
tremors of after shock I feel,
Which are breaking down
my walls brick by brick.

This winding road I now
travel will turn so bleak,
So this strength I must keep,
Without courage I am merely nothing,
So I shall place one foot
in front of the other,
Whilst walking this painful
road to recovery.

Star

A star I see, but you are more.

No that's a woman, hiding in a star.
Which she holds sparks of stardust,
Bringing light to where she's
never been before.

She is just a blank canvas,
Waiting for her story to start,
While she waits for the one,
To create an extraordinary masterpiece.

For her life is now ready to be painted.

Vow

A vow I shall uphold for the rest of my life,
Take my hand run, through open
fields of happiness with me.
Through the sparkling sun,
That makes us dance with glittering rays.

I see more happier memories
we shall make,
Through dancing in stormy puddles.

Never forget to hold me with your warmth,
On them cold winter nights.

Then I shall be with you through
every thunderstorm,
That tries ripping right through you.

The love we have conquered,
Which grows with such flawless pace,
Consumes my entire world.

So I will be her vow forever more.

Wars

So many talk of peace will wars rage on,
A world in constant crisis with one another,
The threat of nuclear wars hangover
the average man's head,
However, the average man
does not care for wars,
For only peace he sees.

The threat made by dictators
we have all seen before,
Which have been revolted by the masses,
As the human race stands separated,
Not knowing what the future holds.

Now the time is upon us to stand,
For the freedom of every
child this world loves,
The children of the world we see,
With pain held so bold in their eyes.

So we should all be looking at a
future with peace in our hearts.

*"Sorrow only possess the minuscule
part of my becoming soul,
But my becoming soul upholds enormous
quantities of contentment insight."*

Uncomfortable

Pins with needles track
through every limb,
Making hands take form of claws,
No spasm goes unnoticed by naked eyes,
As they sit but stare uncomfortably.

Watch a little bit more its ok,
I am just sitting in a glass cage.

For the world to judge,
My body that holds many imperfections,
No one will ever understand,
what happens inside.

For I will show the world,
Then make uncomfortable stares fun.

Never Really Had Your Love

I never really had your love,
Since you left it under lock with key,
So it never came to any damage.

As your heart, you never let
outside your castle walls.
So it would never bleed or become fragile.

For your defensive moat
kept everyone at bay,
You were the Ice queen of emotions.

The rare moments I saw your core,
I fell harder but could never
conquer them walls.

As the closer I came the
harder you shut down,
So I never really had your love.

Alive

Comes the time we all need to travel on,
It's always alone because
we need to heal,
The lands might seem baron,
Only they won't be baron for very long.

Beauty will return to dazzle us once more,
Then at that time we will welcome
it back with open arms,
As this is what we only deserve,
The light to shine upon our lives.

Then breath in every sweet aroma,
The world has to give,
For the world will never let us forget,
How alive we truly are.

"You built your home on wild free land, Like the gypsy girl you saw all them years ago, With scraggly hair but skin and bones so gaunt...."

Venomous Tongue

Throw them insults,
Make yourself feel better,
I am not the only one to blame,.

You have also said harsh things,
You call me selfish,
Your the one out, for your own self gain.

All you've done is judge
everything talked about,
Then continued to hurt me,
With your venomous snake like tongue.

The only thing I remember you saying,
Is rid yourself from this world,
By taking all you have from your own life.

Now I see with clarity,
That I am better off without you in my life.

Erased You

That's what I needed to do,
Erase you from my life,
Piece by Piece so I may move forward,
It has been hard,
As I never wanted to let go.

Now I see it's for the best,
So I will close the book,
On this chapter,
Then store it away in me.

I will never utter your name again,
As you have killed me over time again.

Now I will build my foundations once more,
To start a new book in my life,
For this one will be without you.

We Are Never Alone

Remember we are never alone,
Someone is always guiding you,
You might never see them,
Be sure when you do.

Embrace the new found glory,
They have installed in you,
Then run hard but fast as you can,
With all your might.

Never look back at the life that once was,
Look to the distance,
See the new light in your future,
Spread your wings then soar high,
Always believe in yourself,
This will never make you fall.

*"So delicate her heart she possess,
But her soul must run wild but free......."*

Suicide

No more do I want to live,
For no more do I want this pain,
I just want to be empty from all within,
Now I need to be at peace in my body.

If that means the stars take me,
Then I will shine with them but be free,
Don't be sad or cross,
For I can not cope no more.

I have battled for to many years,
For I am so tired now,
So let me lay my head down,
Then close my eyes,
I will rest in all your hearts.

Till the day we meet again,
I will be waiting for every last one of you,
So I can hold you again,
Therefore, for my last words
I will say I love you.

Then goodnight.

Broken Smiles

Broken smiles is all we see,
People in pain half heartedly smiling,
Trying to be brave but just wanting to cry,
Let the sorrow run down our faces.

There is no shame in letting tears fall,
That only shows strength we hold,
This proves we hide nothing
from this world.

So be strong never suppressing
any emotion,
Then let it flow from every suffering,
We have ever endured without hesitation,
Then we can release
ourselves from the pain.

Saved Me

You saved me,
Brought life back through smiles,
Made me believe,
I could be whatever I wanted.

Gave me courage to fight everyday,
You was always proud,
Held my hand at every hurdle,
To make sure I cleared any troubles.

Talked when moods got the better of me,
But comforted when words had no help,
Always showed me what I meant,
By showing me your love.

As nothing calms me more,
Than you being next to me.

"Words striking the page are the lyrics of my soul, Defining who we really are....."

*Don't judge as you won't understand,
Yes I stand alone in a
fight no one sees,
No one knows the enemies
I shall battle with,
Expect the warrior inside of me,
You will never walk in my shoes,
So please don't try to understand
the pain one carries,
For sometimes the invisible war
is only one person's battle......*

Printed in Great Britain
by Amazon